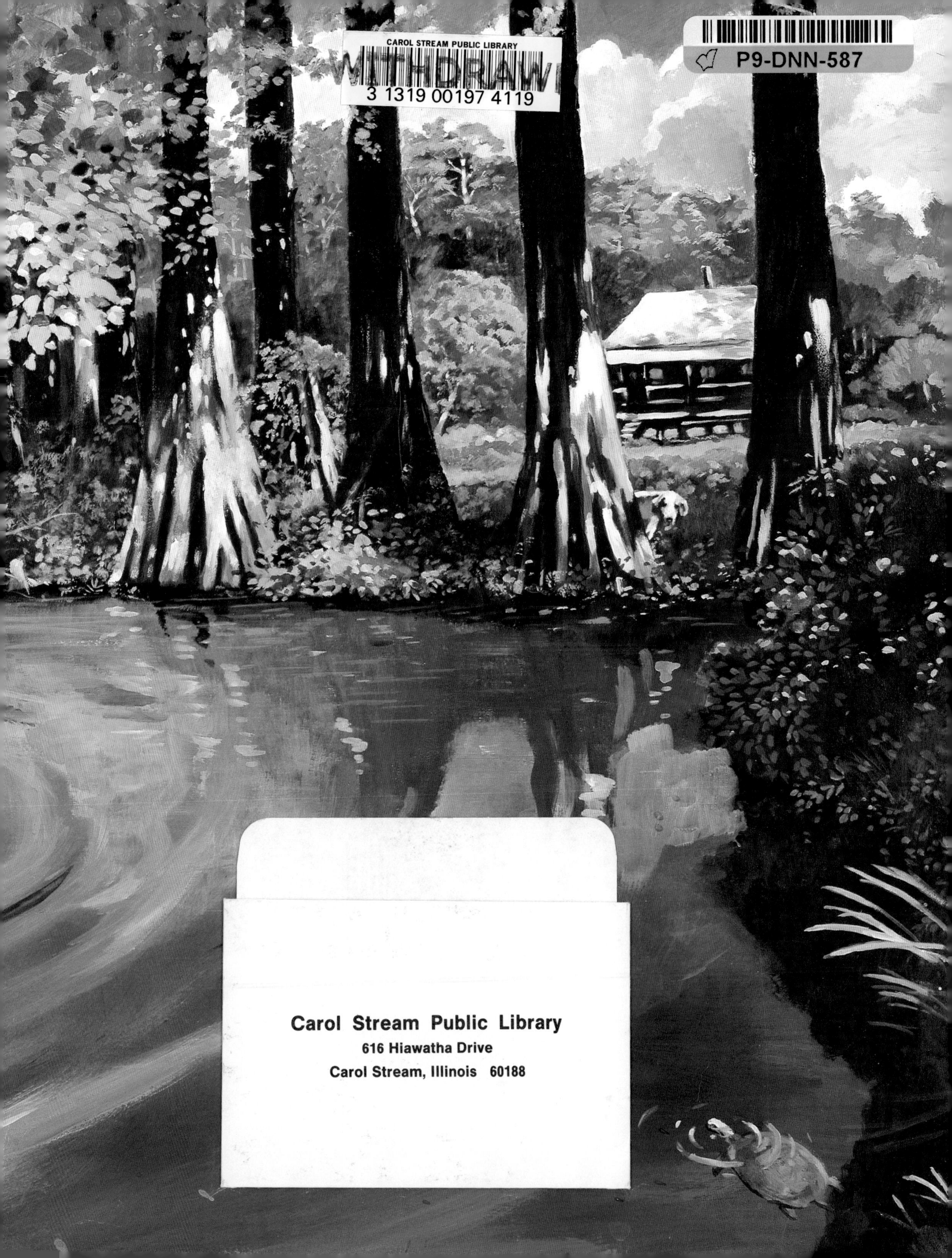

Why Alligator Hates Dog

A Cajun Folktale

J.J. Reneaux

ILLUSTRATIONS BY
Donnie Lee Green

For Tess and Jackson, who know
a thing or two about hound dogs.
— *J.J.R.*

For Sarah, Trena, and Bryan.
— *D.L.G.*

Text © 1995 by J.J. Reneaux
Illustrations ©1995 by Donnie Lee Green

Published 1995 by August House LittleFolk,
P.O. Box 3223, Little Rock, Arkansas 72203,
501-372-5450.

Book design by Harvill Ross Studios Ltd., Little Rock

Manufactured in Hong Kong

10 9 8 7 6 5 4 3 2 1

LIBRARY OF CONGRESS CATALOGING-IN-PUBLICATION DATA

Reneaux, J.J., 1955–
Why Alligator hates Dog / J.J. Reneaux; illustrations by Donnie Lee Green.
     p. cm.
Summary: When sassy old Dog tricks Alligator, king of the swamps, it starts
a feud that continues to this day in the Louisiana bayous.
ISBN 0-87483-412-0: $15.95
[1. Alligators—Folklore.　2. Dogs—Folklore.　3. Cajuns—Folklore.
4. Folklore—Louisiana.]
I. Green, Donnie Lee, 1949–   , ill.   II. Title.
PZ8.1.R278Wh   1995
398.2´09763´0452798—dc20
[E]   94-46965

A Note on Cajun Dialect

Reading and listening to folktales is a wonderful way for children to learn about the world. Not only do they teach us about our differences, they also remind us of our similarities. Children love exploring new cultures. They delight in learning words and phrases of another language. The glossary below is designed to easily acquaint readers with the Cajun words found in this book.

- **M'su Cocodrie** *(Muh-syoo Kō-kō-dree)*: Mr. Alligator
- **ça va?** *(sah vah)*: How's it going?
- **non** *(nōhn,* a muffled sound as in *[lon]g)*: no
- **mon ami** *(mōhn* [as in *non* above] *ah-mee)*: my friend

Take a minute to practice saying the words. As you read the story, be sure to add your own playful touches. If you have fun with the story, your listeners will, too!

— *J.J.R.*

BACK IN THE OLDEN DAYS, M'su Cocodrie was king of the swamps and bayous. He got plenty of respect for true. Everybody was scared of Alligator's sharp teeth and his big tail. Everybody, that is, except for that old sassy Dog.

Every evening, Dog stood on his porch and teased Alligator something awful. He growled and barked and howled.

"Arhooo, M'suuu Cocodrieee, come and get me!
Arhooo, M'suuu Cocodrieee, come and get me . . .
IF YOU DARE!"

Alligator did not dare go after Dog.
He did not want any trouble with the man
who lived at Dog's cabin. M'su Cocodrie could only
thump his tail, snap his teeth, and hiss.

"Someday, that Dog is gonna get too close. And me, I'm gonna snap him up and grind him into mincemeat!"

Now one day, Dog strayed too far from his safe cabin. He was hot on the trail of Rabbit. *Thumpity, thumpity, thump.* Dog came running down the bank of the bayou.

"Oh, *non, mon ami,*" that sly Dog whined.
"I did not say 'Come and get *me.*' I hollered,
'Come and get *it.*' Each evening Man
brings me a big bowl of juicy scraps.
I call out for you to come join me for supper.
Come to the cabin this evening. You
will see for yourself that I have a special
treat for you!"

"Well now, that is just what I am gonna do. You mangy mutt, I am gonna snap you up and grind you into mincemeat!"

Alligator thumped his big tail and hissed. "So, at last you come to visit, eh? Every evening you tease me. 'M'su Cocodrie, come and get me if you dare!'

Dog wagged his tail real friendly-like
and started to whining.
"M'su Cocodrie, *ça va?* How you doin'?"

Shoom, thunk! Dog fell down
the hole! He found himself
snout-to-snout with Alligator.
Dog was in trouble for true.
He knew he better do some fast talking.

Rabbit was smart-smart! She led him right up
to that gator's hole. Rabbit jumped right on over,
but Dog did not see the dark hole in time.